TWEEN TALES

The Adventure

Begins...

TWEEN TALES

The Adventure Begins...

With Contributions from:

Yusuf Moosa Bux, Quraisha Shah, Sara Moosa Bux,
Aadam Dadabhay, Yusuf Asvat, Hana Hoosen,
Sohayb Belaid and Zaheera Jina

YIZ
PUBLISHING

A catalogue record is available for this publication
At the National Library of South Africa.

First Published by YIZ House Publishing
P.O.Box 700, Lenasia, 1820
PRINT: 978-0-620-88286-6
YizHousePublishing@gmail.com

Cover Design: Zaid Ismail
Editing: Dr Zaheera Jina
Typesetting: YIZ House Publishing

Contents

Introduction

It all started with the announcement from President Cyril Ramaphosa on 15 March 2020 that South Africa would go into lockdown as a result of Covid-19. This meant that all children would stay at home 24/7. The option of online schooling was not on the cards as yet. On Monday, 16 March, I made an informed decision to offer an "online" creative writing mentorship to tweens.

I delight at the sight of a superb simile or an equally appropriate metaphor. When I read to my nine-year-old son, we often analyse the figurative language in the text. We marvel together at how authors dress their words to create beautiful writing.

I believe that empowering children with the power of writing good descriptions is like equipping them with knight's armour in battle.

The advert for the tween mentorship was well received and we were in full Zoom from Monday 23 March. Lockdown in South Africa commenced from Friday 27 March. The children were involved, and they earnestly began their craft of rich writing. I involved them in the craft of identifying figurative language in text and using them in their own writing. The twenty-day mentorship also includes storyboarding and character descriptions.

The tweens were eager to write, and as their stories took shape, I decided that I wanted to showcase their writing to inspire other tweens to take up the challenge to write. Tweens are children between the ages of seven and thirteen. Tweens have an increasingly advanced vocabulary and understanding of language. Unlike younger children, tweens have the words to accurately describe those big emotions they're feeling, from furious to passionate to betrayed (Rich[1], 2019).

The creativity of a tween blooms like rosebuds in spring.

Tween Tales: The Adventure Begins includes the creative craft of seven children ranging in age from seven to thirteen-years-old. The collection includes all their creative writing from the course: their poetry, a description titled, "The world outside my window…" as well as a short story of 2000 words.

The collection begins with, The Treasure Hunt; by ten-year-old Yusuf Moosa Bux that sets the scene of a young boy's quest for treasure. From there, I tried to compile a selection of stories that best represents a full range of tween experiences, be they realistic or fantastical. The submissions that I

---

[1] https://www.parents.com/kids/development/parenting-a-tween-is-actually-pretty-great/

received reflect a central focus on heroism and adventure.

Heroism may be the ideal that tweens aspire for themselves. Heroism is about helping others (people and animals), doing the right thing and being recognised for it. For a child, learning about the virtue of helping can only result in good things. This is what superheroes are all about. They are about not staying silent if one sees an animal or another human being needs help. Being a hero is about acting and trying to make the world a better place.

I've arranged the stories in this book to showcase the tween's individual writing creations: poetry, descriptions and stories. Stories include fiction tales of going on a junior ranger camp, saving aquatic animals and realising the importance of family.

Being a Tween involves a playful balance between little and big. This means that they might act silly in one moment, and sophisticated in the next. Tweens have a lot of informed opinions. They know it all! Through the stories they write, we catch glimpses of their world – what they consider embarrassing, what they aspire for themselves and how they strive for independence. But at the end of the day, we know that tweens still need our unconditional love and support.

Tween Tales: The Adventure Begins; is for all the Tweens out there and for us parents who love them.

Dr Zaheera Jina
July 2020

Yusuf Moosa Bux is ten-years-old. He lives in Kwa-Zulu Natal, South Africa. He enjoys playing sports - soccer, archery and swimming are his favourites. He wants to become a soccer player when he grows up.

STORY

The Treasure Hunt

Waking up

It was a hot Sunday morning in December. The Durban sun shone brightly like an orange torch waking ten-year-old Yusuf. He sat up in bed, yawned and stretched out his arms excited for the day ahead. He swung his legs happily off the bed, resting his feet onto the soft marshmallow rug that covered the floor at the edge of his bed.

The duvet on his bed was still neatly spread so with both hands, Yusuf ironed out the wrinkles that had formed during his sleep. He tidied his room and trooped out to the bathroom. The toilet gurgled as water flushed down the cistern. Yusuf washed his hands, allowing soap suds to play on his skin. He grabbed his green alien toothbrush, applied a blob of toothpaste and rhythmically ran the bristles over his teeth in a swift movement. He cupped water into his hands, sipped and gargled. In the mirror, he stared at himself. His short black hair stood in spikes on his head. His eyebrows were thick, and they moved around playfully to the movement of his cheeks – inflating and deflating like a croaking frog. He was dressed in patterned long pyjama trousers and a top.

"Ooh, yummy!" Yusuf exclaimed!

Pancakes

He smelled a very good smell as he brushed his teeth - a smell as sweet as honey from a bee's hive. His stomach growled, and his mouth watered as he raced down the stairs. A smell that delicious can only mean pancakes!

"As-salamu alaykum," Dad said, as Yusuf flew down the stairs. Dad is short, with very little hair on his head, and he has a beard. Yusuf looked past Dad and saw his little sister eating something syrupy. Sara has long black hair that reached past her shoulders, just like her mum's. She is short, like a regular seven-year-old. Mum was flipping pancakes and tossing them into plates like a chef in a 10 out of 10 restaurant. Mum is average height with straight black hair that comes past her shoulders. She was wearing her usual jeans and a top.

Yusuf grabbed a plate with the highest stack and went to the table to eat. He poured chocolate sauce over them. The chocolate oozed everywhere. The flavour exploded in his mouth as he bit into it. Yummy! These pancakes were the best in the world.

Going to the Beach

"Yusuf when you have eaten your breakfast, get ready… We are going to the beach!" Mum said. Outside the cloudless sky beckoned to them

"Yippee!" screamed Yusuf and Sara together.

Sarah and Yusuf raced upstairs to change into their swimming costumes. In his room, Yusuf pulled open his cupboard door and pulled out his green and black all-in-one swimming costume from the bottom drawer. Out tumbled his other costumes and patterned the floor.

Yusuf hurriedly changed into his swimming attire, grabbed his slip slops and dashed into Sara's room to collect his sun-cap, goggles and towel.

"Oops!" Yusuf called out as he collided into Sara, pushing her over. They fell to the floor in a heap.

"Ouch!" Sara cried her screams muffled from beneath the Lycra swimming costume in which she hid.

"I'm sorry Sara," Yusuf said stifling a giggle. He pulled down her costume, and playfully ruffled her hair. "Come on, let's go!"

"Yay! I can't wait!" Sara laughed.

Yusuf and Sara marched down the stairs into the kitchen.

"Have you got everything?" Mum asked. "Buckets, extra towels, caps, sunblock..."

I'll do that!" Sara said, running out the door. "I'll get the buckets!"

"Don't get all the buckets and spades!" Mum cried. "Just two is fine."

"Okay!" Sara yelled back.

She grabbed two of the biggest buckets and four spades, all different bright colours, and ran straight to the car, flinging them into the boot, before racing back to the house.

In the meantime, Yusuf raced upstairs and grabbed a few towels from the linen cupboard. He

stuffed them into a blue beach bag, forgetting to close the cupboards. He did one last check to make sure that he had everything before going downstairs again.

Finally, they jumped into the car, and they were off!

As they drove along, Yusuf was bored sitting and doing nothing in the car. He looked out of the window and saw the monkeys jumping from tree to tree. He saw a flock of glossy starlings, their feathers a dark glossy blue. At last, they reached the beach.

To get the beach, Yusuf had to walk through a path that was surrounded by thickets. The bush looked like a snake would pop out at any time and bite him. He walked carefully, looking out for snakes as he cautiously trailed behind his family.

As soon as he passed the bush, he raced down the rocks and into the beach and started digging.

The map

Yusuf used his hands and sometimes the spade to dig a deep hole in the sand close to the sea. He always chose to dig where the sand was a bit wet. He used the sand from the trench to form a wall facing the sea so that the waves wouldn't destroy his trench while he was working on it.

As he was digging, Yusuf hit something hard. His plastic spade was of no use. I will use my hands to dig around it, and then I'll pick it up, he thought - wondering what it was.

He dug until he could pick the item up. It was a faded clear glass bottle, with a scroll of paper inside it.

Yusuf pulled open the lid and carefully slid out the paper. It looked like a map. Yusuf wondered if

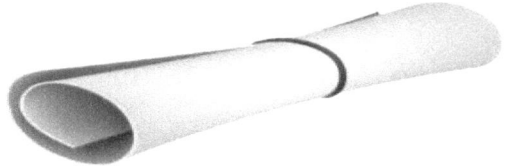

it was a treasure map, with gold as the hidden treasure.

"Mum! Dad!" Yusuf shouted. "I've found something!"

Mum and Dad were relaxing on coloured towels basking in the sun. Yusuf rushed over to them and showed them the map and the bottle.

"Can I see where this leads?" Yusuf asked.

"If it doesn't lead too far away," Dad answered.

"Okay!" Yusuf shouted, and raced off, attempting to follow the directions on the map.

A few minutes later, Yusuf ran back. "The directions are leading me to the road," he told his parents.

Treasure!

"Let's pack up and follow the map!" Dad exclaimed.

They hurriedly collected their belongings and rushed to the car. Dad started the engine amidst Sara and Yusuf's excited ramblings.

The map led them back to their house. The co-ordinates pointed to a spot in their backyard. Dad collected the spades from the shed, and father and son happily set to work. The mid-afternoon sun glistened brightly on a background of a brilliant blue sky. They dug, and they dug, and they dug!

CLUNK! The spade hit into something hard!

"Dad, we hit it!" Yusuf cried.

"Yes, Yusuf! Dig around it, and then we can lift it up."

Yusuf and his Dad dug deeper around the object. Dad got into the hole and hauled the object up into his arms. The box was as light as a feather and the size of a shoebox. He dusted off the sand to reveal a deep brown wooden box with the etching MAX on its lid.

They were eager to reveal the contents of the box. Dad held the box and Yusuf very carefully lifted the lid.

To their astonishment, the box lay empty!

Cars

Yusuf carried the box into the house. From within he felt the rumbles of objects tumbling onto his arms.

"Dad, there's definitely something inside! I can hear and feel it!" cried Yusuf.

Dad took the box from Yusuf and placed it on the kitchen counter. He removed the lid and knocked

on the sides and bottom of the box. The bottom seemed hollow. Dad tried very carefully to remove the bottom of the box. The bottom gave way and out rolled a collection of small steel cars. The cars were classics, and their paint looked faded. Dad's eyes shone with surprise. He picked up one car at a time, admiring the artistic detail.

"Wow, Yusuf! This is some collection! This is a Cadillac, and this one is a Royce! And this one…"

At that moment, the doorbell rang.

The Owner

Yusuf went to see who it was.

Through the peephole, he saw an old man and a small boy. The old man was bald with a short white moustache. He wore a black waistcoat over a white shirt and smart black pants. The boy looked about Yusuf's age, with long black hair

"Hello. Who are you?" Yusuf asked, opening the door slightly.

"My name is Max, and this my grandchild. Many years ago, I buried something here."

"What was it?" Yusuf asked.

"It was a collection of classic miniature cars, and now I'd like to give it to my grandson. I could have come earlier, but he was quite small then. Now he is old enough to take good care of them."

"Come in," said Dad, over Yusuf's shoulder. He had wondered why Yusuf was taking so long and had appeared to see what was going on.

"We found a treasure map on the beach today," Yusuf said. "And it led right here."

"The treasure map!" the old man exclaimed. "Never in my life did I think that someone would find it! And on the same day that I decided to come and get it too! Did you dig it up already?"

"Yes," said Yusuf. "It's right here." He passed the box to the old man who carefully took it and slid out the false bottom.

"Look," he told his grandson, in a hushed whisper. "This is my old collection of cars that I told you about. They are worth a lot of money nowadays."

He slowly pulled one car out and held it up to the light. "It looks just like how it did twenty-five years ago when I decided to bury it."

He turned to Yusuf and said, "Thank you for being so honest."

The man turned to leave. Before he left, he told Yusuf, "I will come back in a few days to give you a reward for your honesty."

The Reward

A few days later, the old man returned, but this time without his grandson. He handed Yusuf a small Cadillac, the one that Yusuf had admired the most from the collection.

"Thank you," said Yusuf. "This is was my favourite one!"

"This was my favourite one as well," said the old man. "This is why I wanted you to have this one. Honesty is always the best!"

POEM

Friendly fish

I see a friendly fish,
floating fast.
I see a fowl with frizzy feathers,
flying fashionably far.
I see a funny frog, feasting on figs.
I see all of this,
when I am fishing with my family.

Quraisha Shah is nine-years-old. She lives in Johannesburg, with her Mum, Dad, and older brother. She enjoys many things including experimenting with her Mum in the kitchen, rollerblading,  gymnastics, reading, and gaming. Pizza and chocolate are her favourite foods. She wants to be an author and have a successful YouTube channel when older. Quraisha is already making her way on to both. Her favourite author is Jeff Kinney who writes the Diary of the Wimpy Kid books.

STORY

Aisha and Omar's Adventures: All That Matters

01 June
Dear diary
Tomorrow is going to be the best day of my life. Tomorrow my family and I are going to Disney World in Florida. I'm so excited. I have never been to Florida before.
Xoxoxo
Aisha

The day has finally arrived. We are finally going to Disney World. Dad promised me that we would visit the Universal Orlando Resort. I would finally get to see the Wizarding World of Harry Potter. I have been looking forward to this for months. When Mum wakes me up at 3 am to catch our flight, I jump out of bed like an

excited jack out of a box. I don't think I slept a wink, but there would be enough time to sleep on the airplane.

"Omar, hurry up!" I scream from downstairs. "You are going to make us late!"

My brother Omar is not excited because he thinks Disney World is for babies. But what do teenage boys know? And my brother was like most teenage boys with his head in a game or the clouds.

"I'm coming stinky bunny," he shouts back. He knows I hate being called that but I'm in such a good mood I just let it go.

Before we board the plane, Dad buys us a bunch of sweets.

"Don't eat them all in one go," Mum warns. I stuff mine into my backpack and race to the boarding section of the airport. When we are finally seated, I take out my phone and my headphones, Omar does the same.

"Are we going to sleep on the plane?" I ask Mum.

"Yes," my mum says in an irritated voice. I guess all that waiting around has made everyone in my family extra grumpy.

"How many hours will we have to be on the plane?" I ask.

"We've been through this a hundred times, Aisha!" Mum answers. "Eight hours." She turns back to her book. Hmph! I fold my arms. I thought that this is supposed to be a holiday, but Mum is already stressed. I roll my eyes and switch on my tablet.

"Aisha, it's nearly nine o'clock you should get some sleep," Mum says.

"Okay," I agree. I brush my teeth in the bathroom and hurry back to my seat next to Omar.

"Omar, tomorrow when we wake up we will be in Florida! Now let's go to sleep!"

"I'm not nine-years-old like you, Aisha. I'm going to stay up and play games on my computer," Omar answers.

"Can I play," I say, building my hopes up.

"No way," says Omar. "Aisha, please just sleep!"

"Fine, then you've left me no choice but to tell on you," I retort.

"You couldn't even if you wanted to because Mum and Dad are sleeping," says Omar. He's right. They would be mad at me for waking them up.

Hopefully, tomorrow everyone will be in a better mood, I think. I snuggle into the cosy warm blanket. I say prayers and drift away into dreamland.

It's my fault! Again!

Omar wasn't joking, when I wake up, he is still playing games. I get a huge fright when I look at him - he looks like a zombie! The rings under his eyes are as dark as two black holes, and his face is as pale as a white sheet. I pray that he is no longer grumpy. I don't want anything to spoil my day. I quickly wipe my face with a wet wipe and get ready for landing. When we wait to leave the plane, my tummy begins to ache.

"Ow-Ow-Ow!" I cry out.

"What is the matter?" Omar asks.

"My tummy is extremely painful!" I cry.

"I wonder why," he says sarcastically. "Must be all the sweets Mum told you not to eat."

Oh no! I might have eaten more than I was supposed to.

"I need to use the bathroom."

"Ouch! Aisha, you look really do look sick!" Omar says.

 I climb over him to get to the bathroom. "Put my phone in my backpack," I tell him, hurrying to the bathroom.

I get back just in time as everyone is getting off the plane. At least my tummy feels better.

"Here's your backpack," Mum says. I grab it as we hurry off the plane and into the airport.

I want to take a selfie to send to my friends back home, to make them all jealous.

I shift all my stuff around my backpack, but I can't find my phone. Mum told us to wait for them as they collected our luggage. Omar is sitting half asleep.

"Omar!" I shake his arm. "Did you put my phone in my backpack?" He sits up and gives me a blank stare. OH NO! I scream in my head. Mum and Dad are going to kill me. This holiday has not even begun yet, and it already feels like a disaster!

I ran up to Mum and whisper to her what has happened.

"Aisha!" Mum says. "I keep telling you to take care of your stuff!" I bite my lip, ready to cry. Mum says that I have to tell Dad. Let's get this over with, I decide.

"Dad, I think I forgot my phone on the plane."

Dad is furious. His face grows beet-red.

"Aisha, why are you still standing here? Hurry! Go with Mum to the lost and found desk!" Dad yells.

We hurried to the desk. And thankfully, my phone sat as though waiting for me, on the desk. I am over the moon get my phone back. *Maybe this holiday will be okay from now*, I think. Mum and I hurry outside.

Dad tells us we just missed the bus to the hotel. I feel so bad. The next bus is in forty-five minutes.

What a jittery start to our holiday!

I'm never talking to Dad ever again

The next day I wake up brimming with excitement.

It's a new day, and I am hopeful for a great day ahead!

I run like a happy toddler into my parent's bedroom - I bounce onto their bed. I behave like a wild, crazy monkey.

"Stop, Aisha!" Dad yells. The only time Dad yells is when he is stressed. Dad is on a call, and I wait until Dad finishes the call. "I'm sorry, Aisha, we have to cancel our plans for today, I have an emergency at work. We can go tomorrow."

What?! No way! Why did we come here if Dad has to work? I'm devastated. I've always wanted to go to the Universal Orlando resort, and now when we have the opportunity to go, Dad's manager goes and ruins everything. I stomp out of the room like Ellie, the elephant in my favourite cartoon.

I complain to Omar. He is so happy, but I feel more upset.

I go to Mum. Mum says that I can't always get my way. Mum explains that these things happen. I start to argue about how I thought we were on holiday and weren't supposed to have meetings with Dad's boss. Mum says that sometimes holidays don't go as planned.

"Don't worry, Aisha, we will go to Disney World tomorrow," says Mum.

I feel a little better. "I'm never talking to Dad ever again," I whisper to myself.

"I can hear you," says Mum.

I pull out my upper lip till it looks like a fat sausage. I spent the rest of the day doing absolutely nothing.

Poor Aisha!

I wake up the next morning, not expecting much from this day.

I walk slowly to my parent's room because I don't want to get my hopes up after what happened yesterday.

"Dad, are we going to Disney World today?" I ask.

"Yes, Aisha."

I twirl around the room like a ballerina. I feel giddy, and my tummy even has butterflies.

"Omar! Omar! Get up!" I scream. "We are going to Disney World!"

"Yay," he says his voice thick with sarcasm.

I dress quickly in my favourite dress with tights.

"Mum! Dad," I cry. "I'm ready to go to Disney World!"

They laugh at me as we all head out. Omar drags his feet.

When we arrive, all I want to do is go to the rides at the Wizarding World of Harry Potter.

"One thing at a time, Aisha," Dad says. "Let's get some snacks first. What do you think?"

"Yes, I want popcorn, please, Dad! Thank you!"

We find a popcorn stand.

"I want the pink Candy Mandy flavour, please, Dad." I point at the writing on the board.

Dad buys the largest bag that he can get. Today is really going to be the best day ever! I hug the bag close to my chest to breathe in the warm sugary aroma. I munch away taking in all the sights and sounds of the world, candy to my eyes. I don't know which thrilling ride to choose first.

The candy flavoured popcorn tastes like a perfect blend of strawberry and vanilla. I throw a handful of popcorn into my mouth. I munch.

"Ouch!" I cry out.

"Aisha! What's wrong?" Mum asks.

I point to my mouth.

"I think I cracked my tooth," I say.

"Let me see," Dad demands.

I open my mouth wide for Dad. I'm afraid, and my heart beats wildly.

"Aisha, your filling has come out," Dad explains.

"Oh, no!" I wail.

"We have to get to a dentist immediately," Dad exclaims. "Or the tooth might break off and create a bigger problem."

"No, Dad! I'm terrified of the dentist!"

"We have no choice," Mum says.

Mum uses Google to search for the closest dentist. Dad calls an Uber.

Mum sees me shivering in the taxi.

"Don't worry Aisha, we all here with you, you are going to be fine," she says.

"Mummy, I'm so scared!" Omar gives me a hug, and I feel an itsy-bitsy better.

The dentist explains that I need a filling. The procedure takes twenty minutes, and I won't be able to eat for a few hours.

I'm sad. I don't want to see Disney World anymore. I just want to go home. I hold Mum's hand the whole time.

Family always

When we get back to the hotel, I'm exhausted. My mouth is swollen, but the pain is gone. I feel like a cloud floating above. Mum tucks me into bed.

When I wake up, I hear nothing. It's too quiet. Did my family go off to Disney World and leave me here? I crawl out of bed and walk to the front room. My family is sitting on the sofa, waiting for me.

"Look, Aisha," Omar says.  He has bought me some makeup and brushes.

I scream, "OUCH!" The pain is back. My mouth is still swollen, so I smile with closed lips.

"You can turn me into a princess," Omar says.

I pinch myself, but no, I am not dreaming. I run to my room and come back with a pretty dress.

"Don't tell me I have to put that on," Omar teases.

"Yes, you do," I nod. My family laughs.

"Okay, Aisha! Just this once!"

"What are we having for dinner?" I ask. "I'm starving."

"We bought your favourite Taco Bell."

I can't stop smiling. "The double chalupa box?"

"Yes," Dad says.

"With extra jalapenos?" I ask.

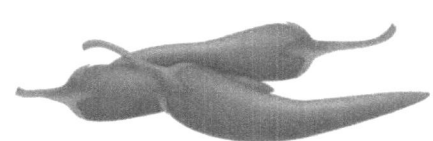

"Of course," Mum says, "When you are done we can watch all your favourite movies!"

Dear Diary
I may have not gotten the chance to go Disney World. But I got to spend time with my family, and that's more than I could ever ask for. I will treasure this holiday forever.
Xoxoxo, Aisha

POEM

The world outside my window

There's a strange world outside,

It's a crazy and a weird place,

Cars zooming around and weird animals everywhere,

Like the other day, I saw a pudgy pig pounding at

 people on the pavement,

Sometimes I wonder why are they are out?

So many planes zooming around,

And so many people pottering about.

The people don't smile anymore,

They don't look at me,

They don't smile at me,

They all look like ghosts wandering around,

And I don't see any children,

A world without children,

Right outside my window,

But the flowers I see are real,

I feel like I can see the flowers putting on pretty
dresses for the world to see,
I love flowers fresh like a rain
in winter,
And trees with leaves I
can see over the red
rooftops of houses,
I see the endless blue
sky,

And sometimes the clouds
smile back at me.
It's the highlight of amazingness,
Sometimes I wish I could stay up late and look out
the window,
Maybe when the moon disappears …
The children will come out.

Yusuf Asvat is nine-years-old. He enjoys solving the rubics cube, building LEGO and playing chess. He has two younger brothers and lives in an extended family home with his brothers, parents, his uncles, his grandmother and Mama. Yusuf wants to become an animator and work for Pixar when he grows up.

Going Viral

Frozen Frog

I was waiting tensely like a frozen frog beneath icy cold water. I stared at the rectangular grey framed clock with large numbers, hanging above the door to my classroom. The big hand very slowly ticked on. My teacher sat at her desk at the far end of the classroom. She was oblivious to my plight. I am Kai. I am a tall thin boy with a neatly trimmed short school haircut. I waited in anticipation for the school bell to ring.

I had a big cricket match that afternoon. We were playing against the Croteas in the semi-finals of the WC tournament. Straight after, I had a swimming gala. There was too much to look forward to, and I couldn't wait! The best part was that Mum would bring the best snacks in the world! Ooh, Yummy! There would be samosas and pies, mini hotdogs and juice freshly squeezed for me! My mouth was a river of sweet saliva – I could almost taste the delicacies.

And then just as I was settling into a dazzling daydream, I jumped out of my skin. TRINGGGG! The bell rang.

I quickly jumped up off my chair. I called out a goodbye to my teacher and rushed like a hunted rhino to my bag which stood against the wall. I hauled myself to the door and battled through the many children who ran around like wild animals. Suddenly something yanked my ankle to a halt. It felt like I had defied the law of gravity that was pulling me down. I hit face-first on the ground amidst charcoal black shoes.

OUCH! I looked up, and to my dismay, I found Toby grimacing down at me. Who is Toby? You may ask. Toby is my arch-nemesis. Toby is tall and muscular with a dishevelled orange crop of hair. He calls me names. He mocks me. I try to ignore him!

I rose slowly, like an injured fly. I trudged. I limped down the stairs pulling myself along like a tug-of-war rope dancing in the arms of excited children. In the vast distance, I spotted Mum with my younger sister, and I saw the large blue patterned swimming bag of goodies. I jived across the field to the far end to meet Mum. Mum stood tall like an elegant swan – her long neck hidden beneath an orange and blue headscarf. Mum always wore jeans and tops with sandals. I hugged Mum. I was so happy to see her.

I grabbed the large swimming bag oblivious to Mum, asking me how my day was. I unzipped it. I rummaged into its belongings. Mum warned me to carefully take out the savoury tub. I lifted the tub. Beneath I spied red cloth with a sprinkle of white polka dots on it.

Pain!

I reached for the cloth. I heaved it out of the bag.

My stomach lurched. It felt like a churning of cheese. I was nauseous; silvery sweat oozed out of my pores. My heart pounded like a hammer knocking nails into wood.

"Kai! What's happening to you?" Mum cried out. Her face full of concern.

The words remained captive in my mouth. They refused to break out. I lifted the cloth for Mum to see.

I watched as Mum's face distort from worry to extreme astonishment. She gasped! Her hand shot out to cover her open mouth, and her eyes looked as though they were stretched open.

"Oh, no, Kai! Oh no…"

My five-year-old sister giggled. Her body shook like jelly in a bowl, and her eyes glistened with mischief.

"Nya! It was you, wasn't it?" I dodged past Mum to grab the little rascal, but she hid behind Mum. Her little fingers danced around her small ears. Her tongue wagged wildly. She moved her head from side to side. "Na-naa-na-naa! You will never catch me," she yelled.

I looked down at the cloth that I still held limply in my hands. It felt as soft as silk. The lacy frills rolled like waves, pricking my skin. I let go, and the material fell to the floor.

Nya lunged for it.

"Kai that's my new swimming costume for when I'm older and you making it dirty!"

Ah yes! The stark reality! I … would … need … to … wear … my … sister's swimming costume to the International swimming gala!

"Kai!" Mum cried. "Quick, hurry! Get dressed! Your cricket match starts in five minutes!"

I ran to the changing room. It was a prison cell. I felt claustrophobic. I changed into my white formal cricket attire. I peeled off my blue school socks. Pain shot like hot lava. I remembered my injured ankle. The skin had thickened and was turning blue. I pulled on my white socks and sneakers. I ran to the cricket field. Phew! I had a minute to spare.

"Kai," Coach yelled. "You on!" Coach was burly. Coach was scary! Coach always chewed on a ten-centimetre long wooden twig.

I usually love being batsman, but today I was really worried. I walked to the wickets, still limping.

"Hurry up, Kai!" coach yelled.

From the wickets, I could see the whole field. The

bowler looked fierce at me in the face. He shot the hard red ball straight towards me. I tried to hit, but I fell forward into a well of pain. My team roared, brandishing me with a storm of insults. I scanned the crowd. I saw Toby laughing. "Looser!" he screamed. I felt horrible. I had let the team down. I missed all the shots. When the match was over, my team was really upset with me. I had disappointed them. We had lost. I felt sad like a toy thrown out of a house.

Diving deeper

I walked slowly to Mum. I plopped down next to her on the newly mowed green grass. Mum tried to cheer me up, but I felt lost like a stray kitten wandering down the street. There were only fifteen minutes left before swimming.

"Mum," I pleaded, "I'm really not feeling well. Please can we go home?"

"No Kai, no! It's the Internationals, and your team needs you!"

"But Mum… I have to wear Nya's polka dot swimming costume! Everybody will laugh at me…"

"Kai, relax. Nobody will even notice. I promise!"

I was so scared.

I felt a shiver travel through me like when you know you are being watched. I realised Toby had been staring at me laughing like he had watched the funniest comedy in the world. I felt so humiliated. Tears welled up in my eyes, but I held them in. I dragged my feet to the changing rooms. He strolled by, passing me, and when he did, he stamped on my foot.

"What's wrong, loser, are you going to cry?" he yelled. I didn't respond. I was afraid that the tears would fall. Just then I looked down at my gleaming silver watch. I realised there were only five more minutes before the swimming gala. I rushed into the large face brick building. The roof looked like it had been torn out of a tin can. Just then I smelt the odour of chemicals heaved from the depths of the hot pool. I continued to the change room. Toby was putting on his blue swimming costume. When he swam, it gleamed like a dolphin frolicking in the depths of the pool.

I unzipped the blue patterned swimming bag and slowly pulled out my sister's costume, hoping that Toby wouldn't see. But he did! He stared! He burst into tears of laughter, but I ignored him. What else could I do? I quickly slipped the costume on pressing the frills down. I wished that they would disappear.

I walked out of the change room still limping from the fall.

The conductor was herding the swimmers to the diving boards.

"Can the under-10s please line up here!" he called.

I got onto the grey-coloured diving board that stood at a slope to the water. It felt wet beneath my feet. I had to keep my balance from slipping off. I felt all eyes on me. I was light in a world of darkness. Suddenly the conductor shot his gun. I dived in feeling the water swoosh around me. I was a spoon gliding into jelly oblivious to the world around me. I gave it my best. Suddenly my head hit the wall. I rose. I felt thousands of eyes staring at me. And then…

Going Viral

Applause rose from the crowd.

I found everybody staring at me and cameras flashed. I shrivelled at the sight of them. I crouched

trying to make myself smaller. I remembered the polka dot costume that I wore.

Then I watched as a man with an all-in-one blue swimming costume walked towards me. His bronze shoes shone brightly with the sunlight that gazed onto them from the square-shaped skylight above us. He handed me a blue first place ribbon. It felt as rough like sand, but at the same time, it was

as flimsy as paper. I climbed out   of
the pool and tried to run to
Mum, but I was forced to
walk with my feet scraping
against the rough stone floor.
Finally, I reached Mum. I
forgot that I was wet. I went

in for a huge hug. I heard Nya shout out,

"Kai, you are wet." I leapt backwards wild like
a lion shot with a paralysing dart. I slipped. I was
falling with my head about to hit the rocky ground.
Suddenly someone grabbed me.

It was Nya.

My sister had saved me.

'Congratulations, Kai," Mum exclaimed. "You
came out first place!"

I was speechless. Shocked! Surprised! I walked
in a daze to the change room. I was still limping
from the fall. I walked past Toby. He stared at me.
He was a choked mouse. I ripped off my sister's
pink polka dot costume. I slipped on black tracksuit

pants with bold white writing and a plain blue t-shirt. When I put on my turquoise sneakers, my swollen ankle howled in pain. I limped out of the change room. Mum waited with Nya at the door to the large building. I saw Mum scrolling on her lush pink phone while Nya played in the soft red sand. I handed the blue swimming bag to Mum. We slowly strolled to Mum's small maroon car. I wondered what snacks Mum had brought for the trip back.

Suddenly Mum screamed. She looked down at her phone.

"Kai! Kai!"

"Yes, Mum?"

Mum lifted her phone to show me the pictures that she was looking at. I stared at thousands of pictures in the rectangular screen of the phone. Photos kept updating. More pictures, all of me!

The comments read #newfasiontrend

I had gone viral!

DESCRIPTION

The World Outside my Window

I took a peek outside my window and what I saw was magical. The shape looked glittery and shiny like the sun reflecting off water. I took a closer look. It was a water bottle that someone had forgotten from the 1950's…

There was something moving inside. *What was it?* I wondered. It looked white as freshly churned cream. I whipped the bottle cap off. With it came a sudden WHOOSH of air faster than the speed of sound. The wind tossed me onto the street. OUCH! It hurt! It felt like spikes piercing my back.

And then I saw it! I watched a rumbling truck rolling down to me!

And then suddenly something pulled me off the road. It was Mum.

"Ziyaad what are you doing? You could have gotten killed!"

"I saw something Mum!" I cried.

"What? A crazy snail?"

"No mum, it was a two centimetre bird. Believe me Mum, I really saw it!"

Mum interrupted me. "You mean that you saw the Esperigear?"

"I think so…"

"How? They are almost extinct!" Mum cried.

"Why?" I asked.

"Because of pollution, don't you know?"

"Of pollution?"

"Why do you think that we couldn't get you a turtle for your birthday?" mum asked.

"Are they almost extinct as well?" I asked. Mum nodded.

"If I help pick up litter Mum," I asked, "Will my helping to clean the world, heal the world?"

"Yes, honey… It will!" Mum smiled.

Sara Moosa Bux is seven-years-old. She lives in Kwa-Zulu Natal. She enjoys painting, swimming, gardening and riding her bike. She enjoys writing her own story books.

Superheroes to the Rescue

The Mystery Begins

The smell of warm, syrupy waffles drifted through the air. Amahle took a bite. "Mmm … too delicious!"

Amahle, superhero detective, loved waffles. *At least there are no mysteries to solve today*, she thought. I can enjoy my waffle with ice cream and golden syrup.

"Did you hear about the robbery that happened earlier today at the diamond store?"

"No, I didn't!" a woman shrieked in reply.

"Something was stolen! The most special diamond in the world!"

Amahle held her fork in mid-air as she overheard the conversation from the table next to her. Her friend, Mrs Meg, was the diamond store owner! *So much for no mysteries*, she thought to herself.

In a flash, Amahle gobbled up the rest of her waffle and hurried out the door. She rushed back home, her orange and gold shoes glistening in the lamplight of the streets as she ran.

She reached home, flung open the door, and flew into her room. She changed into her superhero costume: a green pants, top and goggles, with a long silky gold cape.

She flew downstairs to the telephone and dialled her friend's number. Someone on the other end picked up the phone.

"Can I speak to Layla please?" Amahle asked.

"Sure, I'll call her."

"Layla, there has been a robbery at the diamond store! You've got to meet me there immediately! Wear your superhero outfit and hurry!" Amahle said.

"Okay, I'll be right there… but I may take a minute or two…" said Layla.

"Bye-bye, I'll meet you there in a minute or two," said Amahle, and hung up.

Amahle flew to the diamond store, and sure enough, Layla was there, waiting for her. Mrs Meg was outside the store. She saw the two girls and unlocked the door for them.

As they carefully prowled around the store, something caught Amahle's eye. "One clue down!" Amahle shouted.

The Clue

A footprint right where the stolen diamond had been! Layla skipped over and took a photo. The footprint tread was very strange as it had a triangular pattern.

"This doesn't look like a construction boot," said Amahle.

"Let's follow the footprints!" Layla said excitedly

They followed the footprints out the back door, through the alleyways, and down the street.

It took them towards the outer area of the city. It was darker than midnight, and the night felt scary. There were absolutely zero stars in the sky, making it feel spooky. The footprints lead them down a trail to different places. They ended at a paved area that spread out to different trails leading to various cabins.

Layla and Amahle were a bit confused. But they would take all it took to solve the mystery.

They began to try to solve the puzzle. It was so hard. "Let's go back," Amahle said. "Yes, let's go back," said Layla. As they flew back home, something clicked.

Amahle had an idea.

The plan

Amahle explained her idea to Layla. "We will invite everyone who lives in the cabins for a party. It will be a spectacular party."

"Well," said Layla, "How will a party help us to solve a mystery?"

"We are going to have not just an ordinary party, but a special type of party. Everyone will have their own section of mud. They will write their name and address on the card by their section. They will all need to put one foot into the mud pit. Then once everyone has left, you will match the footprint

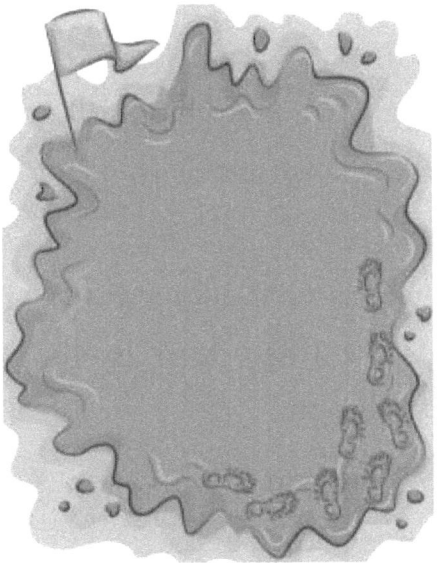

to the photo from the diamond store. Then we are going to deal with the culprit."

Amahle and Layla made invitations and dropped them off at the cabins. They made sure to ring the doorbell after dropping off the note and race away.

The Plan in Action

The party went according to plan. The guests arrived and jumped in their mud pits. As soon as they left, Amahle and Layla went to Mrs Meg's house.

"We know who the culprit is!"

Mrs Meg was surprised. "How?" she asked them.

They explained about the party and their plan.

"But," asked Mrs Meg as she looked at the card. "*Who* is Sam?"

"Good question," said Layla. "We're about to find out!" she squealed.

Amahle and Layla flew back home. The policeman, Mr Bob, arrived. He was a short, round man with no hair. They quickly went to the cabin. Layla went down the chimney, while Amahle stood by the front door, the policeman at the back door.

Amahle knocked on the door.

Sam opened it. "Come in," he said.

Then the policeman knocked on the back door. Sam went to open it.

"Hello," said Sam.

Just then, Layla flew down the chimney with her cape fluttering behind her.

Mr Bob, Layla and Amahle raced up the stairs. Sam was right behind them to see what they were up to. They opened up one of the drawers, and there stood twelve gold and silver diamonds. They gasped. Just then, quick as a flash, Amahle grabbed the ID that was on the table. She opened it and checked the name.

Mr Bob read it aloud. "The Shadow!" he exclaimed! "We've been looking for him for years!"

Sam, who was actually, *The Shadow*, tried to creep down the stairs, but Layla swooped over his head and blocked his path. He tried to go back, but the policeman stopped him. He tried walking to the side, but Amahle stopped him. He was triangle like his footprints! Mr Bob arrested *The Shadow* and took him to jail.

"You'll be staying in jail for the rest of your life!"

Stolen Items

"What are we going to do with all of these stolen items?"

Mr Bob had an answer. "You need to return the things to the people who are here and alive. The rest of the items you can keep."

"It looks like he had been stealing for quite some time now. And here is Mrs Meg's diamond!" Layla exclaimed.

"We can give everything to charity," Amahle said.

Amahle and Layla skipped excitedly around. They helped the policeman take *The Shadow* to jail. Then they went to return the diamond to Mrs Meg.

"Wonderful! You found the diamond!" Mrs Meg exclaimed. "You really are very clever detectives."

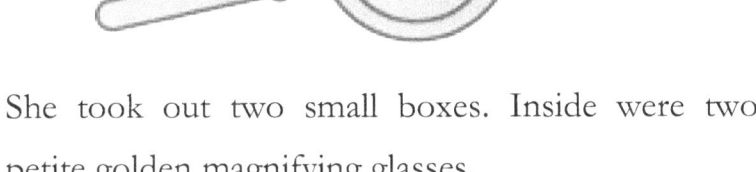

She took out two small boxes. Inside were two petite golden magnifying glasses.

They sparkled and shone.

"These are for you. Thank you for all your help, Amahle and Layla," she said, as she handed them a box each.

One Month Later

One month later, Layla swung her legs off the side of her bed.

She flew out of the yard and went to buy an ice cream. Luckily for her, she didn't have to go far. The ice cream shop was right next door. She asked for an ice cream with three scoops and went back home.

When she reached the house, Mr Bob and Amahle were waiting outside. Their faces held serious expressions.

"What's wrong?" Layla asked.

"The Shadow has escaped!"

Amahle and Layla flew back to the jail cell that *The Shadow* had been in, and sure enough, it was empty. There were a few personal belongings that

The Shadow had left. They saw grease from the jail cell that spread all the way out the back door, through the alleyways, and into the inner part of the city, the city of Nukemex. As they followed it, it stopped outside a small, tiny doorway. The doorway led to different houses. They couldn't use their same plan, because *The Shadow* would realise what they were trying to do and say he was sick.

So they decided to go to one of the houses. Amahle could send her drone. Her drone had a camera. So she flew her drone through the area over the chimneys, and she saw a woman and man and a few kids.

"That is definitely not the Shadow," Layla said. "It must be the other cabin." She swooped her drone over the trees, and with a tiny flick, it flew into the chimney and right down. On the screen, she saw a man that looked like *The Shadow*.

"Yep," said Amahle, "It's him!"

"Yes," Layla and the policeman agreed.

"Shh… can you hear?" Amahle whispered? "He's on a video call. Listen and to what he's saying, and look at who he is talking to."

A lady with long black hair tied up in a ponytail filled the screen. "So, are you coming with me to the secret place," she said in a high pitched voice.

"Of course," replied the Shadow. "Pick me up in fifteen minutes."

Amahle, Layla and Mr Bob looked at each other. "Uh oh," Layla said. "He's up to new tricks again, like before."

"You're right," Amahle said. "He is up to something, but I have a plan."

Amahle shape shifted into the black-haired ponytail woman who they had seen on *The Shadow's* phone – his friend.

Amahle crept inside, before flicking her drone towards Layla and the policeman. When *The Shadow* saw her, he smiled. "You came!" he said.

"Yes, I came!" said Amahle, in a high voice. "Let's go to the special area that no one knows about. It is full of treasure," she said.

"Yes, I'm ready to go. Let's roll!"

Amahle took out a pouch. "You will need to wear this thing that is inside my pouch. Close your eyes."

Captured forever

The Shadow closed his eyes. Amahle opened her pouch and quietly slipped a pair of handcuffs on him.

Then she shed her disguise. "Now!" she shouted

Layla came flying out from the chimney, and Mr Bob came through the door. They all surrounded *The Shadow*.

There was a knock on the door. In walked, the Shadow's real friend. She gasped at the scene.

"Oh no, you don't!" she shouted.

Layla was too quick for her. She pulled out a pair of handcuffs and snapped them onto the girl's hands.

Mr Bob grabbed the two criminals, packed them into his police car and drove them to a ship which transported them to prison on an island far out in the ocean. It was impossible to escape from this cell.

Epilogue

Two weeks later, Amahle and Layla were having coffee and ice cream. The coffee was as hot as fire.

"OUCH!" Layla cried. "That coffee burnt my tongue."

"I don't think you should have it right now," Amahle said. "Why don't you start with the ice cream instead?" Amahle bit into the ice cream. It was chocolate ice cream, with delicious pieces of mint. The chocolate melted in her mouth.

"At least there are no more mysteries to solve for now."

"Yes," Layla smiled. "Until the next one..."

POEM

Grey-haired Granny

I see a grey haired granny,

with a glittering grater,

grinding guavas in the sun.

POEM

What I see from the great hill

I see a goat,

going through the grove,

gulping green grass.

I see a great gorilla,

glaring through a gate.

I see a glowing girl,

grinning.

I see all of this

from the great hill.

POEM

Yeliyand's rooftop

I see a yellow yo-yo bouncing through the air.

I see Yumnah yawning in the yard.

I see yummy yolk on the yacht.

I see Yahya yelling at a yak,

"You get back!"

I see all of this from Yeliyand's rooftop.

Aadam Dadabhay is eight-years-old. He lives in Gauteng and enjoys archery, reading and playing with his toy soldiers. He regards himself as being special because he is named after the first human that ever lived and because he has citizenship in two countries.

THE DINO GROUP

The Noise

A noise, as loud as the sound of twelve lions roaring simultaneously, thundered through the desert plains of Dinocore, in the country of South Amca, where palaeontologists were digging. The cloudless sky was as blue as a bright turquoise sea. The plains of Dinocore were scorching hot. The brown square tents providing shade to cover the excavation site shivered as the sound struck them.

The three palaeontologists at the Dinocore excavation site covered their ears with their hands and, in shock, sprinted in three opposite directions as fast as lightning bolts. One ran straight, one ran right, and one ran left. Coincidentally, they looped around not quite seeing where they were going and comically crashed into each other.

This noise was like no other. It carried a radioactive chemical called dinosaurian. When someone heard it, it affected them by giving them the abilities of a dinosaur. These three palaeontologists who heard the thunderous noise were the first to be affected.

As the palaeontologists lay on the floor, sore and stunned from their collision, they felt something unusual happening to them.

The first palaeontologist was confused as little armoured plates that felt like tiny sharp mountains grew all over his back. The plates were grey with shiny bits of purple and green. He also felt a clubbed tail with the same colours emerge from his lower back. His skin turned the same shades as his tail. His confusion turned into glee, and he exclaimed "Hey! This club tail would be nice to play golf with...except I don't like golf. I think I should call myself Anklyo-Man because these plates and tail resemble an Ankylosaurus!"

The second palaeontologist looked down at himself with concern. "Hey guys, do I look like I'm growing a brown and black tail, longer scaly legs and razor-sharp claws on the ends of my toes and fingers?"

The other two examined him and replied, "Yes, you look like an Allosaurus!"

Excitedly he declared, "Then my name should be, "Allo-Man!"

The third palaeontologist knew he would be next. Within the next five minutes, he had large sharp triangular plates like enormous slices of pizza sticking vertically out of his spine. His tail had four spikes poking out of each side like arrows. "Should I name myself Stego-Man?" he queried aloud.

"That's it!" responded the other two.

Instead of feeling scared by the changes happening to them, the palaeontologists were delighted. They were obsessed with dinosaurs and amazed at the fact that they now looked like and had the abilities of dinosaurs.

Discovery of the Ambassadors

A few days later the three friends were walking on a back road in Go-side City. The road was as quiet as a shopping mall at midnight.

The people of South Amca adored dressing up in crazy costumes to the extent that sometimes they even put costumes on the animals of their country. It wasn't unusual to see horses walking around farms with face paint, and their manes styled and dyed to make them look like lions. Go-side City was known for its love of dinosaur costumes; therefore, the Dino group blended in well.

Out of nowhere, three men with dinosaur features and characteristics appeared, swinging on ropes like monkeys swinging on vines. Unfortunately, the ropes were a bad idea because they were so heavy that their ropes snapped. They tumbled to the ground like dominoes, hitting into each other and landing in a heap on the ground. When Aklyo-man, Allo-man and Stego-man looked at these people closely, they realised two things.

One, it seemed that these men had also been affected by Dinosauria and had developed the features of a spinosaurus, a triceratops and a diplodocus.

One of the men was a greasy grey colour, unusually large with sharp claws on his toes and fingers and his teeth jagged like a rocky hill on a beach. His most noticeable feature was that a giant fin stuck out of his back like a silver sail. He resembled a spinosaurus. Another of the men was humongous with scaly brown skin, a long whip-like tail and a diplodocus neck that was as long as eight bricks stacked on top of each other. The last man was the size of an ordinary person, but he was purple and grey and had a circular frill around his neck that was made of reptile skin. The most remarkable thing about him was that three ivory horns were poking out of the front of his huge head like icicles. The icicle horn in the middle was smaller than the other two, just like a triceratops.

The second thing that the Dino group realised was that they recognised these people; they were ambassadors from the country of Oak. The Dino group had met the Ambassadors when both groups had visited the dinosaur museum in the city of Backback the week before the palaeontologists went to Dinocore. Even though they looked different from before, the Ambassadors original human features were still recognisable.

The Battle

The Ambassadors had been sent to South Amca to speak to the President to ask for technology to dig up dinosaur bones. They threatened that if South Amca didn't give Oak its technology, then Oak would destroy the country of South Amca. When the President of South Amca refused to agree to their request, they decided to attack Go-Side City first.

On their way to Go-Side City, they too heard the thunderous noise that the palaeontologists had heard and had also developed dinosaur powers. Now they planned to use their powers to destroy Go-Side City and all of South Amca.

The Dino Group greeted the Ambassadors warmly and helped them up off the floor. "Hey, aren't you guys the ambassadors from Oak? Welcome to Go-side City" said Anklyo-man cheerfully. One of the ambassadors from Oak barked, "Do you think we are here for a little visit like tourists?! Nope! We will not tolerate anything more from this horrible country! We will crush your city, and you shall die! Hahahaha!"

Stego-man and Allo-man were as shocked as a baby who has his first lick of a lemon slice. They expected to be friends with the Ambassadors because they obviously all shared the same dinosaur powers. Ankylo-man replied to the Ambassadors "You are mischief-makers! We will not let you do anything of that sort!" He turned to Stego-man and Allo-man and roared, "Brothers, let us stop them!"

A battle began with an explosive growl from each side. The horned Triceratop Ambassador charged straight for the Dino Group with his head down like a rushing rhinoceros. Stego-man jumped forward and whipped his spiked tail towards the speeding Ambassador. His tail slapped into the Ambassador's forehead, cutting it and stopping the Ambassador's assault. The Spinosaurus Ambassador sprinted forward as speedily as a cheetah. With his sharp claws, he slashed at Anklyo-man's back like an aardvark digging a hole. Anklyo-man's protective armour acted like a metal shield and saved him from injury. As the Diplodocus

Ambassador stomped the ground to create an earthquake, Anklyo-man swung his clubbed tail around like a wrecking ball and used it to knock all the evil Ambassadors down.

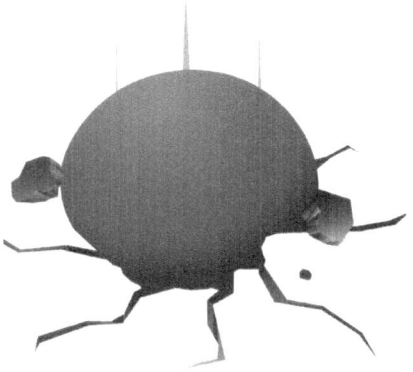

The battle was over, with the remaining Ambassadors wailing all the way to the President's chambers as they were transported for execution. As for the Dino-group, they hosted a huge supper to celebrate the country being saved. Oak, on the other hand, called together a Council of War.

POEM

The Cuckoo Crazy World

I see a creative caracal catching a canary.

I see a cute cat cuddling a crane,

I see a car climbing a clock that is going tick-tock,

And all the things I see are cuckoo crazy!

DESCRIPTION

The World Outside My Window

I sat in my chalet in the Caracal National Park as I watched a caracal pounce up and grab a guinea fowl mid-flight.

As I saw a roaring lion leap out of the bushes, the caracal jumped into the air before the lion could reach it. The lion took the guinea fowl to feed its cubs and the caracal ran off frustrated. The game drive vehicle screeched to a stop to pick me up from my chalet.

I hopped in like a caracal. The game drive vehicle sped off like a cheetah because we were being chased by a lion. Before long, the vehicle slowed to its normal pace because the lion stopped chasing us.

The vehicle crept along, stalking animals, headlights searching the vents - its nose sniffing the air. We heard a rhino shout out in English, "There's a poacher!" and it started stampeding towards us.

Before anyone knew anything, the rhino's horn went straight into our vehicle. Everyone went flying into the air.

"Aaaaah!" they screamed. I fell on the floor.

Black out!

Everyone asks me what happened next when I tell them this story.

I say, "When I woke up, I was lying in my bed."

And that, my friends, is the end of our story.

DESCRIPTION

The Old Man

The old man sat cross-legged on the sofa like a person doing yoga. His beard was as long as a horse's tail and as white as snow. His hands and face were as wrinkly as raisins. He read his newspaper like a man who has nothing to do except read. The children sitting around him were as happy to be there as a thirsty horse who hasn't had anything to drink for two days is happy to be at a water trough.

Hana Hoosen lives in Gauteng, South Africa. She is a thirteen-year-old girl. She has three siblings: an older sister named Rumaanah, an older brother named Mizan and a younger brother named Sami. She also has a best friend named Judi. Hana often helps her mum in the kitchen to prepare meals. She also enjoys gardening, drawing and painting. Hana aspires to become a Designer when she grows up.

Bronze Zebra National Park Adventure

Going away

TRING-TRING! It's my alarm. I woke up feeling a magical wave of excitement flowing through my body. I sat in bed, noticing the stillness of the morning with the occasional rumbling of cars outside. I rushed into the bathroom and went for a shower. I got dressed. I wore my brown rangers t-shirt with the

embroidered Kudu on the top right-hand corner. I
dressed my legs in a pair of blue jeans. I had cleaned

my room in the evening before going to bed to
make it easier for my older sister to tidy up when
she got up. I got ready for my Bronze Zebra
National Park adventure. The strong smell of hot
coffee caressed my senses. I went to the kitchen and
saw Mum preparing breakfast. Mum was a koala
bear, and I gave her a warm hug.

"Asalaamu alaykum, Mummy," I said.

"Wa-Alaykum salaam, Hana. Did you sleep
well? Are you excited for today?" Mum smiled.

I glanced around the large kitchen seeing the
white granite tops like rich almond icing covering
the brown wooden cupboards. The white porcelain

tiles stand in harmony with the modern décor in the kitchen. A vintage round two-seater table adds warmth to the kitchen, and an elegant black shiny chandelier falls from the ceiling and floats above the round table.

Mum was preparing oats which she scooped into a glass bowl – baby bear's - the kind that Goldilocks had gobbled from. I took a seat at the

breakfast nook. The tall steel chair with bright African print backrest welcomed my weight with a soft groan. Mum and I enjoyed a bowl of oatmeal together. Over breakfast, we eagerly discussed the plans that lay ahead.

I had packed my single hard shell white coloured bag into the boot of the car the night before. A habit we learnt from Dad to ensure that we do not forget anything. Wise Dad! I opened the courtyard gate, and Mum reversed the car out. Our car is an elephant and has room enough for us four siblings and my parents. I jumped into the passenger seat and quickly buckled my seat belt. The spring sun slowly peeked out from between the clouds. Mum drove the car down the quiet streets

of Lenasia to the white and green striped bus which stood waiting for us outside Park Primary School.

In the near distance, I could see my friends Saajeda, Nancy and Natasha. I scanned the crowd looking for my friend Nomawethu. I couldn't see her. Mum parked the car on the pavement, and I jumped out. I grabbed my bag from the boot. Mum handed me my brown leather backpack, which held all the food goodies for the trip. I hugged my friends while Mum greeted the senior rangers – Aunty Sylvia, Uncle Abbas and Uncle Ahmed. They assisted us in putting our bags into an enclosed cave in the bus. We were so excited about the trip that we stood together like a crowd of toddlers eating ice-cream. Nomawethu had still not arrived. It was so unlike her to be late. Uncle Ahmed kept looking down at his wristwatch.

"Come on, kids," Uncle Ahmed called. Let's board the bus; we need to be on our way!" We greeted our parents and climbed into the bus. Uncle Patrick, the bus driver, greeted us warmly. My friends and I swooped into a three-seater in the middle of the bus. I sat sandwiched between Natasha and Saajidah. The bus groaned to a start and rolled forward.

Oh no! Nomawethu had still not arrived, and we had left her!

The Journey

Our long journey to Bronze Zebra National Park had begun. I looked around me. I saw chocolate brown floors. The steel-framed seats were covered in royal blue checked linen-like material. All the seats were occupied with other fellow junior honorary rangers. The boys and girls sat together with friends. The senior rangers sat towards the front, and Uncle Ahmed sat in the passenger seat alongside the driver because he had the navigating device.

We all glanced out the window in excitement. The scenery was composed of a bright, beautiful sky with clouds as fluffy as cotton balls. The lustrous sun left little strings of sun rays in the sky.

We started chatting about the activities planned for our trip. We still had not heard news about Nomawethu. Natasha is Uncle Ahmed's daughter, so she volunteered to ask her Dad. She waddled up front like a penguin on a moving glacier. She steadied herself using the iron bars on the seats.

We could not hear her conversation. After some time, she waddled back to us.

"Guess what guys! You got to hear this!" Natasha exclaimed. Her eyes grew large in excitement as she spoke. "So here's the story. Apparently, Nomawethu's younger brother misplaced the house keys…"

"So does that mean she is not coming?" I interrupted.

"Good news is that she is coming. Her parents will bring her!"

"Yippeee! That's great news!" we screamed.

We all felt very relieved. We couldn't wait to see Nomawethu.

My tummy groaned signalling I was hungry. I hauled the brown leather pack bag into my lap. We opened it and found a hoard of snacks: sour punks,

savouries - my mum even packed us a few bottles of fizzy drinks. My hands stretched out and greedily snatched the sour punks. We relished the sticky red sugar-coated candy strips. Oooh, delicious!

I watched Saajidah sucking the sweetness off her fingers.

"Eeeuw, Saajidah! Mum probably packed a pack of wet wipes," I said. I reached into the brown bag and rummaged through its belonging. I spotted the bright yellow small packaging and with sticky hands, pulled it out. I peeled off the sticker on the pack and pulled out three wet wipes. I handed them to my friends. We wiped our fingers clean. Natasha collected our dirty wet wipes and dropped them into a black garbage bag that was tied to one of the seats.

We looked up to see Uncle Ahmed hovering tall in front of us. He announced that we were going to have a short bathroom break. We stopped at a Sasol gas station. Some of the junior rangers went to the bathroom while others went to the convenience store.

Soon we were back on our way.

Trapped

After a long journey, the bus came to a heavy holt. We watched Uncle Ahmed rise like a lion from his seat up front. Silence!

"Rangers we have finally reached our destination!" Uncle Ahmed called out. The silence broke with excited screams and shouts from the rangers.

I looked around. In front of me, I saw a green board with a kudu sign saying Bronze Zebra National Park. Uncle Patrick drove through the gates, and the bus stopped in a green field of grass.

We collected our belongings - we looked under the seats of the bus, we made sure that we had not forgotten anything. I walked to the front of the bus and bounced off the steps into the full sunshine. Emerald green grass formed a blanket at my feet. I looked up to see large mighty mountains creating a bold silhouette. The mystical mountains were a foundation for trees and shrubs to grow.

"Wow!" I exclaimed.

We unloaded our luggage from the trunk and followed Aunty Sylvia to the dormitories where we would sleep during the trip. There was one dormitory for girls and one for boys. The dormitory was a large grey building with black marble tiles on the floors. On the walls, there was a waterfall habitat painted on. Single beds were lined in single files of two beds in a row. On entering, we were presently greeted with a surprise.

"Nomawathu!" we all shouted.

Nomawathu was equally excited to see us. We hugged her, and we told her about our trip.

"The trip was so long!" exaggerated Natasha.

When all the girls were in the dormitory, we discussed our sleeping arrangements.

"We will take the last five beds," Nancy decided. Aunty Sylvia addressed the house rules: we had to make our own beds every morning, keep the dormitory neat and tidy at all times and lights out at 10pm.

After settling in, we walked to the communal room where lunch was being served.

"Ooh, yummy!" I cried.

The rich aroma of biryani embraced our senses. Our stomachs complained in anticipation of being fed. The lunchroom was large with bright white walls and white slate tiles. There were long two-pole bar lights that lit up the room. Six-seater plastic tables wobbled like jelly when we sat down. The chairs were white heavy duty and plastic. We walked to a larger table where the food was laid out. There was a huge pot of biryani, and I experienced a strong scent of cardamom when I dished out my food into reusable plastic plates.

After our meal, the rangers alerted us to a hike that we were embarking on. This specific hike is called the mushroom trail because on the trail there are wild mushrooms growing. Piled in twos, we climbed a steep rocky mountain. The grass was short, and there were certain stones painted white set out to mark the trail. A noble and fragrant Jacaranda tree caught my eye standing tall with its silky bark - its mauve colourised flowers were the dreamiest sight. The sound of chirping birds adorned my ears.

Suddenly my ankle got caught. I tried to

dislodge it while my friends went ahead without me. My foot would not budge. I looked down. I saw roots growing out of the ground like a tangled spider web. I bent down and battled against the wooden chains. Then I saw it. I saw a thick mustard coloured rope with a weave pattern on its surface. It lay there. Still like. I desperately tried to dislodge my foot. Beads of sweat caressed my forehead. My heart pounded like the galloping hooves of a thousand horses; I was petrified. I had lost the group.

And then it moved. It rose. I looked into two beady black eyes with streaks running down the eyeballs.

And then I felt a gush of pain run down my leg.

Revelation

I woke up early the next morning. I heard the wind gently rustling the trees outside as if they were whispering to each other. I looked around me. *What had happened to me?*

Vague memories float around in my head, and I felt an excruciating pain in my right ankle. I looked down to find two punctured holes. My ankle was crimson red and swollen. Nancy, followed by Nomawathu, Saajidah and Natasha slowly stirred and rose. They filled me in on all the details that had happened. A little while later, Aunty Sylvia entered the dormitory.

"You had quite an experience yesterday, young girl!" she exclaimed. "How are you feeling now?"

"I have pain around the ankle."

"You will heal quickly. You were lucky that the snake was not venomous!" Aunty Sylvia then showed me how to clean the wound with an antiseptic solution. She then carefully draped my foot in a soft surgical bandage.

After, I went for a shower and changed into a fresh pair of camouflage trousers and my ranger's T-shirt. I was late for breakfast, so I ate alone. I placed a slice of delicious toast onto my plate. I spread a curl of butter and watched as the butter melted. I topped the buttered toast with a big scoop of smooth raspberry jam. I then poured tangy orange juice into a reusable plastic cup

I later joined my friends in the communal room with my notebook and pen because we were going to have a lesson on snakes and snake bites. Uncle Ahmed was happy to see me. The other junior rangers cheered my health. I felt very shy, and later my friends told me that I had turned beet red. Uncle Ahmed gave us a Snake 101 lesson. It was intensive. I learnt that my snake wears the name Aurora house snake and is one of the most exquisite snakes in the country, favouring grasslands and fynbos feeding mainly on rodents, frogs and birds.

After the lesson, Uncle Ahmed told me that he had informed my mum about my experience and that I should call her to speak to her. I could hear the worry in Mum's voice. Mum sounded as concerned as a lost baby bear's mother.

"Hana!" Mum screamed. "Are you okay? Must we come to pick you up?"

I told her that I wanted to stay and that I felt better. We chatted for a little while. I hung up and returned to the dormitory. In the course of that day, I gradually felt the pain disappear.

During the days that followed, we went rock climbing; we toured to discover dinosaur eggs and footprints in the reserve. We admired San art which

is a traditional art that dates back 1200 years back created by an African tribe. The paint was made out of natural resources. What we enjoyed best of all was the marshmallows on sticks which we melted on dancing flames from evening bonfires.

And then the trip was over. On that morning we left for home the sun slowly raised up while doing so its magical light danced across the sky. We arrived to the smiles of our eager parents. We had too many tales to tell.

POEM

Magical Moon

I see a misty magical moon moving over mountains,

I taste mustard flavoured muffins with mince,

I hear a monstrous mouse moving through in the misty midnight,

The hairy horse halted in the hall.

DESCRIPTION

The world outside my window

The rain drizzles down the window, pitter-patter - my breath makes a faint fog on the cold glass. Across the road I see a dark blue silhouette and a rolling bank of misty grey fog. A water droplet trickles down the window. I look up and see the dark clouds moving apart. I see rays of sun tingling out like a topaz stone on a necklace. The super shiny sun is out yet it is still raining a magical colourful stripped rainbow! The street slowly lights up with life.

Sohayb Belaid is a ten-year-old kid who is in grade four. He was born in Johannesburg, South Africa and he lives in Canada. He loves drawing and buying stationary. He enjoys playing video games with his friends. Currently he likes Fifa and Minecraft. He wants to be a comic book artist when he grows up.

STORY

The Adventures of Fred

Fred's early life

Once upon a time, there was a boy named Fred. He was born inside the boiling hot core of the earth. It was as hot as the savannah dessert times a hundred million. On the day of his birth, there were lightning flashes and the thunder growled in rage. Fred rose from the earth's centre and landed in Antarctica as a young boy of ten. Fred felt freezing cold in his new homeland. He found animal skin to cover his whole body except for his face. He found a large wooden stick which he wore inside a belt. He looked like a polar bear.

Fred had black hair and brownish black eyes and was of medium height. At the time he was slow as a turtle but as smart as Einstein. He portrayed weird facial expressions – he sometimes stuck his tongue out and pointed his eyes in two different directions. In Antartica Fred made friends with the polar bears and learned polar from them. Every day he played with his friends. When Fred saw a polar bear he would run as fast as a cheetah, and jump over the iceberg to greet the bear.

"Boobaaabaaajeebagh waaaaa!" he would say in Polar. This is a greeting. Fred loved life in Antarctica - he  had no responsibilities like school, chores or work.

When he was hungry he dived into the water to get fish, and at bedtime he cuddled closely with his polar bear friends. It was a tremendously, stupendously, amazing life!

Fred's adventures in Hawai

Then one day a big blizzard came and broke the iceberg they were standing on. The blizzard made a huge crack on the ice berg. It sounded like this CRACK-SCREECH-CRACK-BOOM!

It separated him from the polar bears.

The polar bears were on one side of the iceberg and Fred was on the other side. Fred was screaming and yelling and saying a ton of things in polar. They started separating from each other and Fred jumped to grab baby polar and managed to throw him over to the side of mother polar but Fred fell into the frozen water. The water was as cold as Neptune (-1788 degrees).

He was unconscious for a while and when he woke up he found himself in Hawaii. Fred had no idea where he was as he had never left Antarctica. He was stranded in the middle of the ocean as he cried for help and yelled in polar, "UKFhhhiukthgbgfvfcfhguerghnjakUGJGHRHU!" A captain on a ship nearby noticed arms waving in

the water. He took out his kayak and rowed toward the arms. When he realised that the arms belonged to a human being, he grabbed hold of Fred's arm and dragged him to his kayak and they went to the boat.

The captain asked Fred, "Why are you here, how did you end up in the middle of the ocean, Sir?" Fred was just groaning and moaning in Polar.

He was dripping wet and cold. He was shivering and shaking sharply. The captain gave Fred a sweater and a track pants, and offered him some hot chocolate, and Fred felt a warm tingle run up his spine.

The ship sailed toward an island and docked there. They both got off the boat and stood together on a spectacular brightly lit sandy beach. The sun shone down on the sand. There were tall coconut and palm trees. Fred could see the branches moving from side to side. He saw people surfing and playing on the beach. Fred was curious to know what was going on.

He said "GUY-GUY!" to the captain and started walking off.

After three minutes he came to a place where there were tall building, shops, lots of people and noise. Cars were honking. He was downtown in Hawaii.

Fred and his new friend, Omar

Fred walked down the middle of a busy street. Suddenly a grumpy old man driving a big Jeep raced towards him at 120km/h. He was about to knock into Fred.

Fred stared at the car, and did not know what to do.

Just then, a boy rushed onto the street and pushed Fred out of the way.

"What are you doing, why are you on the street, what is your name?" The boy asked.

"Feeed," Fred replied.

"Is your name Fred?" the boy asked.

"Wessss!" laughed Fred.

The boy's name was Omar. Omar had brown, curly hair, black eyes and he was very funny. Fred and Omar became friends and did everything together. Omar told Fred all about gaming and how he won a Minecraft championship.

They played video games; they ate cookies, drank soda and told each other jokes.

The tornado

One day, while walking in town, they saw a fancy, big, new shop with television screens in the window. They stopped in front of the store window, and stared at the TV. They wondered what was going on. A news channel popped up and they watched it. It showed big and small polar bears being separated by a big blizzard.

"Bats me," said Fred. He meant "that's me!"

"Oh no Fred that's you?" Omar said. He gave his friend a sad hug and patted him on the back.

"Wešssssss!" said Fred sadly.

The scientist on the TV said that there was a star above them that night. This was a special star called the 'realm star'. The realm start looks like a regular star, except there are a 100 000 small stars connected to it to make a big star. The realm star sucks up whatever is beneath it, and kicks it out into a different realm. The scientist warned that this star causes trouble and if you ever see it, you have to run away.

Fred and Omar got scared and a cold shiver ran up their spines when they heard this. Omar felt sad for Fred because now he understood how Fred got separated from his home.

Fred had super hearing powers, and he could understand all animal languages. Suddenly, Fred heard the seals screeching and screaming and above them.

"Heeergh, beeeergh!" they screeched. They were saying, Fred please, come to the ocean!

Fred grabbed hold of Omar's arm and they ran as fast as lightning, all the way to the beach. The whales and dolphins told Fred to strike the ocean with his stick. Fred did that and suddenly a big tornado grew out of the water and sucked up every single creature. Fred and Omar's legs lifted up and they started flying and swirling inside the tornado.

Then the terrifying, treacherous tornado tore across the ocean at top speed and went all the way until it disappeared.

After a long while, the tornado landed on some ice and spat out all the creatures.

Fred and Omar landed right next to baby polar bear.

Fred was home and he had a new friend with him

POEM

Sssssssssss

The slithery, silver snake,

named Sohayb,

slept on a sailing

spaceship,

soaring over South

Africa..

The sailing

spaceship sped through

the sky,

and landed in a safari park,

in Southern Columbia.

It then made its way,

to the super sea and,

saw a ship with a sailor,

who was speaking to a small seahorse,

named Sam!

Zaheera Jina has been described as a writer; an academic and a stay-at-home-mum. She holds a PhD in mathematics education from WITS University, South Africa. She is the editor of two books (Saffron and Riding the Samoosa Express) and the author of Surprise! and the StimuMath programme for Pre-schoolers. Zaheera lives in Lenasia,

South Africa with her husband, three sons and many in-laws.

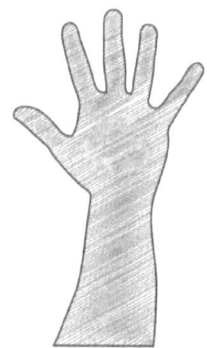

STORY

Green Fingers

I sit alongside my Daadi on the prickly green grass. I'm dressed in gardener's clothes. Today we are planting coriander seeds in the bottom half of a two-litre plastic bottle. First, Daadi puts in sand. The particles are course to my touch.

"Crush the egg shells and mix the pieces into the topping soil, Isa," she says.

"Why egg shells, Daadi?"

"Birds won't eat the seeds if there are egg shells in the topping soil."

Daadi knows all the tricks of planting. We throw banana peels into the rose beds because the potassium is nutritious for the roses. Fruit peels and vegetable shreds go into the compost heap. Potato peels are not good, so we throw those into the dirt bin.

I mix the crushed egg shells into the soil and pour it on top. Lastly, we place the seeds and gently pour water over them. Dad says that Daadi has green fingers, and I agree. Daadi's garden is a colourful collection of plants and mini-beasts that she cares for and grows on her own.

For days now we have been watching a caterpillar change into a butterfly. Daadi says this change is called metamorphosis.

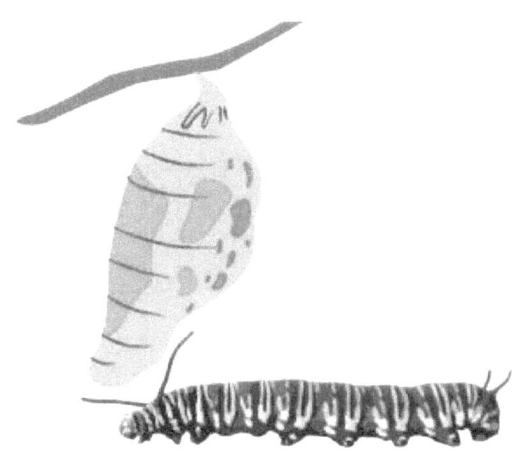

I tell my teacher about the magical world in Daadi's garden. My teacher says that I have an enquiring mind.

"Metamorphosis" and "enquiring" are two new big words in my vocabulary.

"Isa, all of Nature's creatures grow," Daadi tells me.

I often wonder about that. I am growing taller and some of my trousers are too short for me. My brother Yusuf is already nine years old. My baby brother, Zakariyya is also growing and is no longer a baby. He is two years old and I am almost six years old. Zakariyya is daring and wants to do everything I do. He takes out the milk carton from the fridge and spills milk all over the floor. I suppose my teacher would say that he also has an enquiring mind.

"Watch, Isa," Daadi whispers quietly. The chrysalis where the caterpillar is hiding cracks open slowly, piece by piece, until an orange and black butterfly comes out. The butterfly rests for a while, drying its wings, and then flutters away. Daadi says that all of Nature's creatures are born, grow, and then move away. Birds do that, too. They migrate to warmer places during winter. The stray ginger cat that slept in our sandpit also went away. My Dad's sister, my Aunt married my Uncle Waseem and now lives in a different house, far away from ours. I wonder who I will grow up to be. Will I go away? I don't want to.

My Mum sometimes says that we will need to move away to another house, where there are better schools. That makes me feel sad. We have always lived with Daadi. My parents moved in before we were born. Daadi says that when I was a baby, I loved to crawl around, exploring the magical world in her garden. She says I used to watch the snails slide slowly off the wall behind the roses, into the grass. I am afraid that if we move away, the new garden 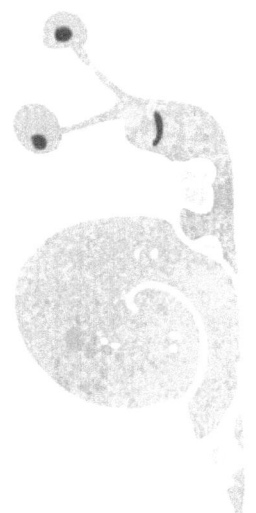 will not be as magical as this one. I am also afraid that I will be all alone there.

We place the coriander seeds we have planted next to the other pot plants. We will care for them and watch them grow every day. After three weeks, I will gently snip the coriander leaves,

and Daadi will wash and chop them finely to garnish the mince for samoosas.

"Look, Isa!" Daadi cries out. On the wall, watching us is a grey and white cat. She jumps down from the wall and walks to the sandpit. She curls up on the sand. Our stray cat has returned to her sandpit home. I can hear laughter coming from inside the house. My Aunt has come to stay with us for the holiday. I decide that it will be okay if I go away, too, because I can always return home, to Daadi's magical garden.

I know that when I am older, I will grow green fingers like my Daadi. I will care for Nature's plants and mini-beasts. There is so much more to do and see. I will create a magical world in every garden that I work in.

Acknowledgements

This year 2020 has been immensely challenging for all. We pray for a better tomorrow! Aameen!

I am grateful to the Almighty for designing our paths in making this publication possible.

I am thankful to all the tweens who did the creative writing mentorship with me and to their parents who grow and support them.

A special thank you goes out to: Yusuf Moosa Bux, Quraisha Shah, Sara Moosa Bux, Aadam Dadabhay, Yusuf Asvat, Hana Hoosen and Sohayb Belaid.

Own your craft; dress your words and keep writing…

With Thanks,
Dr Zaheera Jina.

www.ingramcontent.com/pod-product-compliance
Lightning Source LLC
Chambersburg PA
CBHW030538130626
46552CB00006B/2326